DATE DUE

PIGWIG
and the
PIRATES
JOHN DYKE

METHUEN
LONDON · NEW YORK · SYDNEY · TORONTO · AUCKLAND

A *Webb&Bower* Book
Edited, designed and produced by
Webb & Bower Limited, Exeter, England

This edition published in the United States
by Methuen Inc., 733 Third Avenue,
New York, N.Y. 10017

Library of Congress Cataloguing in Publication Data
Dyke, John, 1935—
  Pigwig and the pirates.
  SUMMARY: Pigwig not only rescues his nephew from pirates,
but returns with the pirates' treasure.
  [1. Pirates—Fiction.   2. Pigs—Fiction.]   I. Title.
PZ7.D9895Pj 1979   [E]   79-13788
ISBN 0-416-30121-5

Printed in Hong Kong by
Mandarin Publishers Limited

On a summer's day by the sea
a little sailing boat called the *Bonaventure* was bobbing over the waves.
Pigwig was steering. His wife, Matilda, sat in the middle
and right at the front was Northcliff, their nephew.

Northcliff's mother, who had lots of children,
had lent him to Pigwig and Matilda for the holiday,
providing he always wore his scarf.

'Remember," she fussed, "weather is weather,
and you've got a weak chest."

That afternoon they were sitting on the beach in the sunshine
watching the seagulls swooping overhead,
when a strange ship sailed into view.

"Yippee! Pirates!" shouted Northcliff. "Can I be a pirate, Uncle Pigwig?"

"Pirates are bad," said Pigwig. "Besides, I don't suppose they're real pirates." But real or not, the strange ship sailed in and tied up at the jetty.

The crew began their spring cleaning.
They scrubbed and polished the ship from stem to stern
and when that was done they hung bright flags from the masts.

Curious people began to gather around the pirate ship.
"Ahoy there!" shouted the pirate captain.
"Come aboard a real pirate ship and meet her jolly crew!"

"Please can we go on the pirate ship, Uncle Pigwig?
Can we? Can we?" begged Northcliff.
"It would be fun," added Matilda.

"Well, it would be very interesting," Pigwig agreed,
"and it seems safe enough."
So they joined the other visitors
walking up the gang plank to the ship's deck.
Northcliff squeezed to the front
and disappeared.

But what a nasty shock! The pirates *were* real! The visitors were
taken down to the deepest, darkest parts of the ship, where they were robbed
And there was worse to come.
After losing their purses, jewellery and wallets,
the poor visitors were made to walk the plank —
Splash! Splash! Splash! — and swim for their lives!

The soaking wet people, dragging themselves out of the sea,
looked back at the pirate ship sailing away.
The pirates were roaring with laughter.

And from high in the rigging,
the tiny voice of Northcliff
could be heard shouting,
"Look at me, Uncle Pigwig. I'm a pirate!"

"Oh dear," sobbed Matilda.
"Those wicked pirates
have stolen poor little Northcliff.
What shall we do?
What will his mother say?"

"Never mind, my dear,
I'll think of something," said Pigwig.

Wasting no time, he pushed his boat out from the beach and climbed in.
"I will rescue Northcliff," he promised bravely. "Goodbye Matilda."

"Goodbye, goodbye, Pigwig," cried Matilda, as she waved her soggy hanky.
And Pigwig set off in pursuit of the pirates,
sailing the little *Bonaventure* as fast as it would go.

Meanwhile Northcliff had been discovered on board the pirate ship.
"Shiver me timbers and slit me gizzard," said the pirate captain,
"if it ain't a stowaway!"

"I'm a pirate, too," said Northcliff.

"And a juicy one, I'll be bound.
Why, you can be cabin boy
to Captain Orrible Gruesome.
Can't he, lads?"

"Aye, aye, Sir," yelled the pirates.

Northcliff was given a broom
and pushed into the captain's cabin
to sweep the floor.
"It's fun being a pirate," he thought.

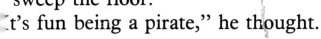

The pirates' mischief had only just begun.
Next, they used a lighthouse for target practice.
The lighthouse keeper was beside himself with rage.

"You villains!" he cried. "Look what you've done to my light!"

"And they've kidnapped Northcliff too!" shouted Pigwig,
who was racing after the pirates as fast as he could go.

The pirates celebrated their good shooting with
a wild Rumpety, which is a sort of party.
They drank lots of rum and danced and sang,
"Rumpety, Rumpety, Rumpety," all over the ship.

Northcliff sang "This little pig went to market" all by himself.
But when he heard the pirates talking about apple sauce and crackling,
he decided it was time to go home.
Northcliff was about to jump off the ship,
when he was caught by the hairy fingers of Orrible Gruesome.

"Help! Help!" squealed Northcliff. "I want to go home."

"You're much too small to swim so far," said the captain.
"Give him extra rations, me hearties, we'll soon have him
fat and ju . . . eh, um, begging your pardon, I meant big and strong."

"Boo hoo! I want to go home," cried Northcliff.
But the pirates only laughed and locked him in the parrot's cage.

The pirates sailed on.
They zigzagged through the busy shipping lanes and caused lots of accidents.
When Pigwig arrived on the scene there were shipwrecks everywhere.

"Look what the pirates have done!"
wailed the captain of one sinking ship.

"And they've kidnapped Northcliff too!" shouted Pigwig,
who was sailing after the pirates as fast as he could go.

At last the pirates got tired of shipwrecking.
They sailed off to find some new mischief.
They left Pigwig far behind, but he didn't give up.
It was easy to follow their trail of skullduggery.

"The pirates have ruined our nets!" cried the skipper of a trawler.
"Now we can't catch any fish."

"And they've kidnapped Northcliff too!" Pigwig yelled back,
as he passed by as fast as he could go.

Meanwhile, Captain Orrible Gruesome had spied a rich man's private yacht.
The people on the yacht were very rich, too.
They were having a fancy dress party.

"Stand by to board ship," commanded Captain Orrible Gruesome.

The rich people on the yacht thought that the pirates
were guests in fancy dress, like themselves.

But the pirates cleverly robbed the people as they danced and capered.

And when their treasure chest was full,
they took it back to their own ship and sailed away.

"Robbers! Cheats!" cried the poor rich people. "Give us back our things."

But the wicked pirates only laughed and jeered.

"Ahoy there!" shouted Pigwig, when he saw the unhappy guests.
"Have you seen any pirates pass this way?"

"Yes!" they shouted. "We've been robbed by them."

"They've kidnapped Northcliff too!" cried Pigwig,
who was still racing after the pirates as fast as he could go.

67109

BONAVENTURE

At nightfall, Pigwig saw the pirate ship lying at anchor
in the bay of a tiny island.
Unseen by the pirates, he sailed the little *Bonaventure* alongside,
tied it up, and climbed on board to look for Northcliff.

"Uncle Pigwig, it's you!" exclaimed Northcliff in delight.
"I knew you'd come."

"I'm sorry I took so long," said Pigwig modestly.
"Now stay close to me young fella, we're going to find that treasure."

"Yippee!" whispered Northcliff.

They followed the pirates' tracks across the island.
From a hiding place they could see the pirates busy burying their loot.
Orrible Gruesome was marking a cross on his map
to show where the treasure was buried.

Then the pirates started another wild Rumpety,
prancing and dancing, shouting and singing
all over the island,
until at last they fell in a heap exhausted,
and were soon fast asleep.

"Now's our chance," whispered Pigwig.
He crept quietly forward and took the
treasure map and pen from the captain's pocket.
Then he wrote something on it and carefully put it back.

"What were you doing, Uncle Pigwig?" asked Northcliff.

"It's a puzzle for the pirates when they wake up," Pigwig replied.

Very quietly, they dug up the treasure.
Very carefully, they filled in the hole.

Then Pigwig and Northcliff carried the treasure chest to the
Bonaventure and sailed away from the island as fast as they could go,
while the pirates lay sound asleep.

When the pirates woke up and looked at their map,
they couldn't understand it.
Clever Pigwig had put crosses all over it,
and it was impossible to tell which was the right one.
Their confusion soon turned to anger as they dug holes all over the place.
But of course they didn't find the treasure.

Although Pigwig and Northcliff had left the island far behind,
they could still hear the shouts and sobs of the pirates.
Orrible Gruesome cried loudest of all.
"Boo hoo! I can't find me treasure anywhere. Boo hoo! Boo hoo!"

And the pirates dug and dug and dug,
until there were so many holes in the island that it sank —
Glug! Glug! Glug! — along with all the pirates.

It was a very happy homecoming for Pigwig and Northcliff.
News of how they tricked the pirates had already arrived.
The people cheered and a band played, "Hail the conquering hero comes!"

"Welcome home, dear," said Matilda,
who cried and laughed at the same time.

All Northcliff's family was there, too.
He had a lot to tell them, but first he said to his mother,
"I wore my scarf the whole time."
And she gave him a big hug.

Pigwig and his wife Matilda are spending a happy summer holiday at the seashore, along with their nephew Northcliff.

One day a strange ship sails into the harbour. "Ahoy there," shouts the captain. "Come aboard a real pirate ship and meet her jolly crew!"

And that is when the trouble begins. Undaunted by disasters and difficulties, the brave Pigwig manages to outwit the villainous pirates in a spirited tale of adventure on the high seas.

As in his previous PIGWIG, John Dyke has created an exuberant picture book, full of inventiveness and humour.